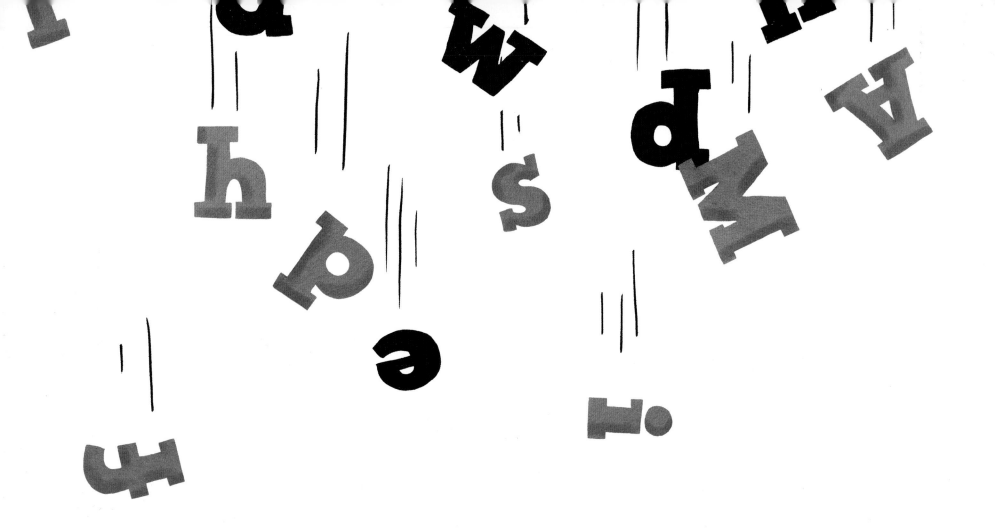

Amy the Red Panda Is Writing the Best Story in the World. Text copyright © 2017 by Colleen AF Venable. Illustrations copyright © 2017 by Ruth Chan. All rights reserved. Manufactured in China. For information address HarperCollins Children's Books, a division of HarperCollins Publishers, 195 Broadway, New York, NY 10007. www.harpercollinschildrens.com Watercolors were used to prepare the full-color art. Library of Congress Cataloging-in-Publication Data is available.   ISBN 978-0-06-233848-8 (trade ed.)   17 18 19 20 21 SCP 10 9 8 7 6 5 4 3 2 1

First Edition

 GREENWILLOW BOOKS

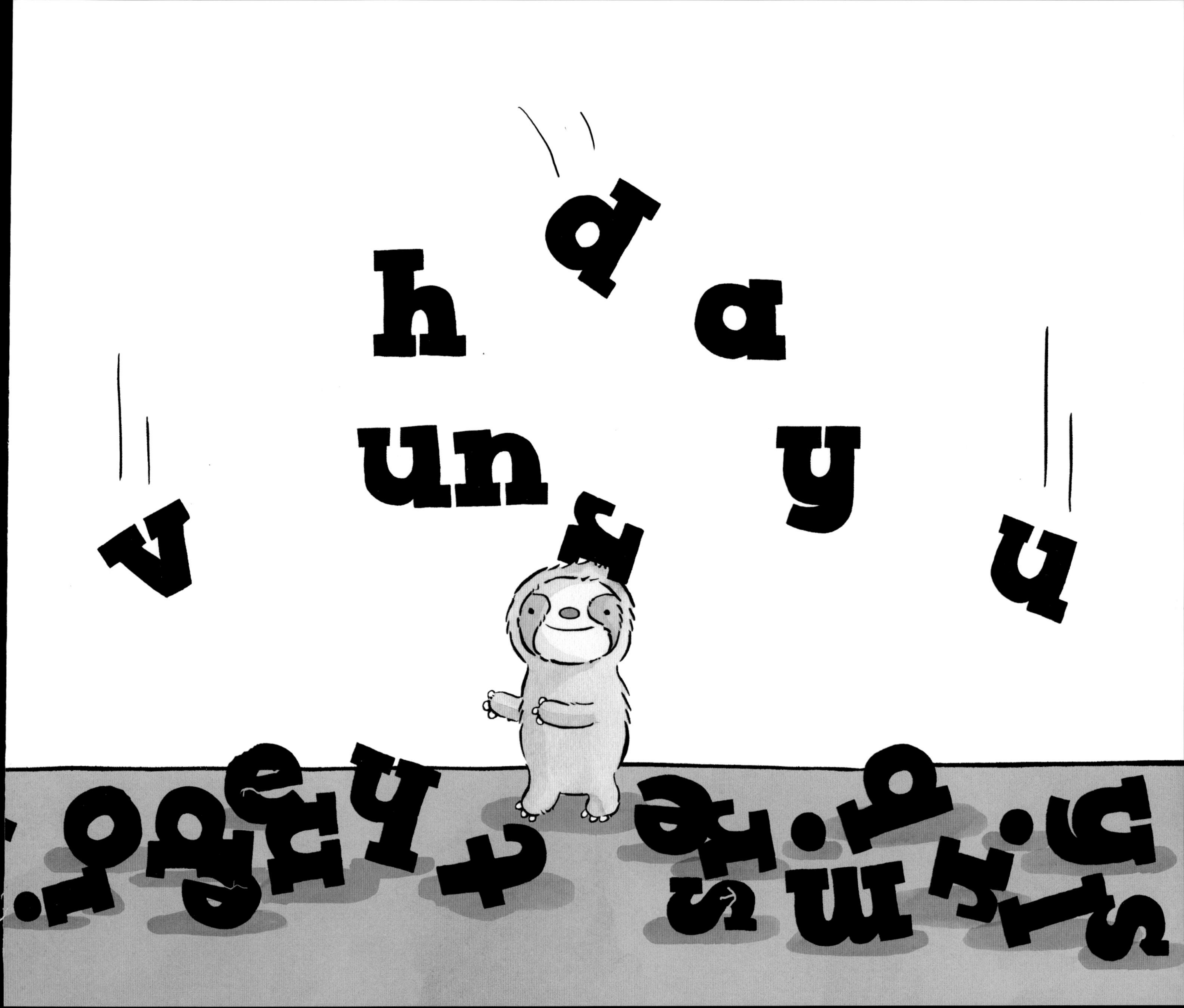

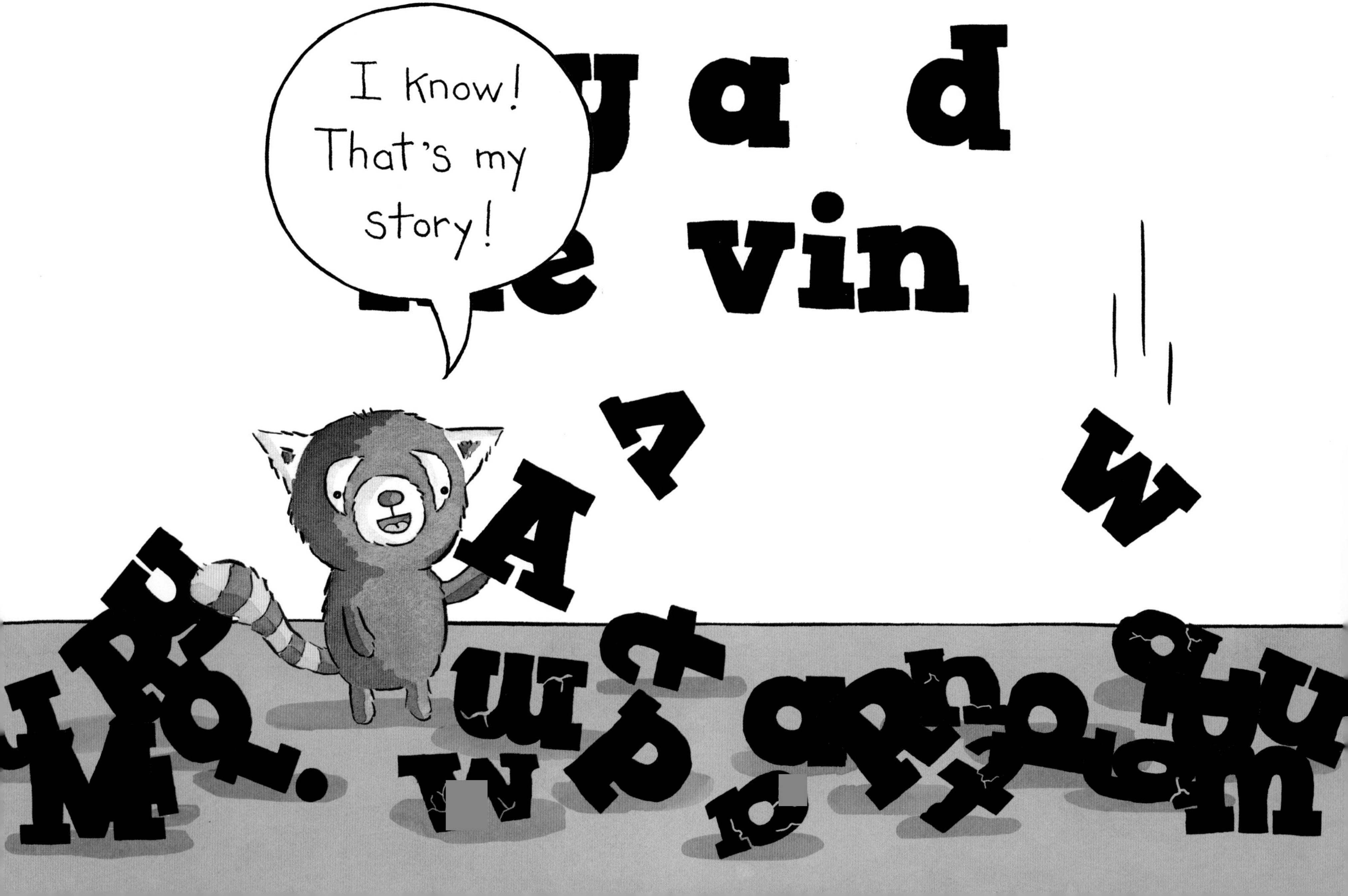
I know! That's my story!

ha a a

funly ly

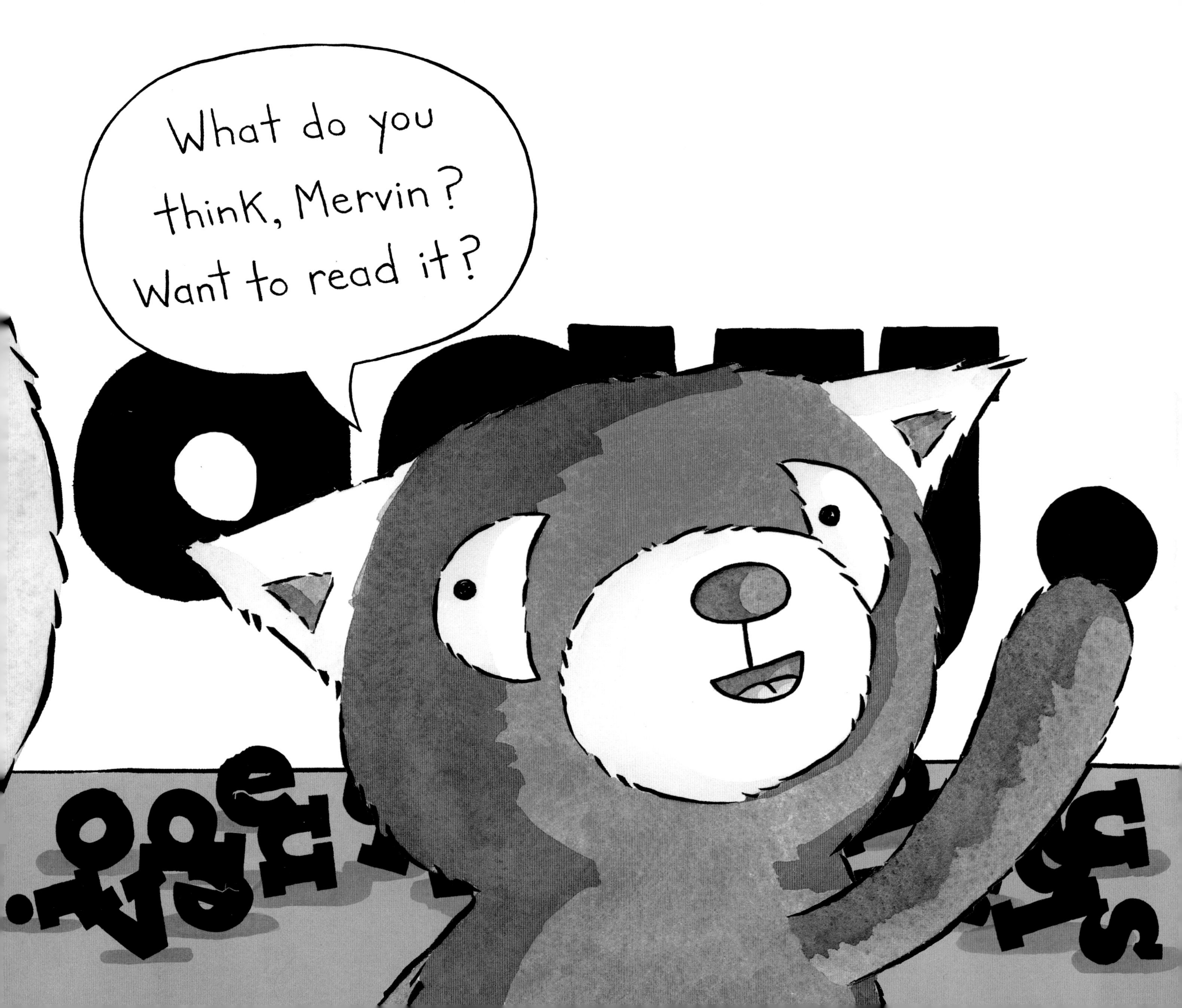
What do you think, Mervin? Want to read it?

Amy and Mervin

had a fun day.

Hey, I really like this story!